the seriously
SPOOKY
joke book

PUFFIN BOOKS

the seriously SPOOKY joke book

KAY WOODWARD

PUFFIN

PUFFIN BOOKS

Published by the Penguin Group
Penguin Books Ltd, 80 Strand, London WC2R 0RL, England
Penguin Group (USA), Inc., 375 Hudson Street, New York, New York 10014, USA
Penguin Books Australia Ltd, 250 Camberwell Road, Camberwell, Victoria 3124, Australia
Penguin Books Canada Ltd, 10 Alcorn Avenue, Toronto, Ontario, Canada M4V 3B2
Penguin Books India (P) Ltd, 11 Community Centre, Panchsheel Park,
New Delhi – 110 017, India
Penguin Group (NZ), cnr Airborne and Rosedale Roads, Albany, Auckland 1310, New Zealand
Penguin Books (South Africa) (Pty) Ltd, 24 Sturdee Avenue, Rosebank 2196, South Africa

Penguin Books Ltd, Registered Offices: 80 Strand, London WC2R 0RL, England

www.penguin.com

First published 2004
1

Text copyright © Puffin Books, 2004
Cover illustrations copyright © Chris Garbutt, 2004
Text design and illustrations copyright © John Fordham, 2004
All rights reserved

Written by Kay Woodward

Made and printed in England by Clays Ltd, St Ives plc

British Library Cataloguing in Publication Data
A CIP catalogue record for this book is available from the British Library

ISBN 0–141–31870–8

CONTENTS

GRUESOME GHOSTS

Shivers running down your spine?
Chill-out with our
ghoulish gags.

What did the
rude ghost
say to the
ice-cream seller?

'Give me
a lolly
or
I scream!'

Where did
the ghostly archer
keep his arrows?
They were all in a quiver.

What do ghosts say to each
other when they can't hear
what's being said?
'Spook up!'

Where do ghosts
keep their scary novels?
On a BOOKshelf.

What do you call a
ghostly police officer?
Inspectre.

Did you hear the one
about the ghost relaxing
in the fridge?
He was just chilling.

3

How did the ghost
frighten crowds of people?
With a loudspooker.

How do ghosts send
letters to far-off countries?
By scaremail.

What do ghosts wear
in the rain?
Kaghouls.

BOO!

What do you call a
ghost's mum and dad?
Transparents.

Where do ghosts
go on holiday?
Scareborough.

Who was the star of the
scary cocktail party?
The ghostess with the mostess.

6

What type of music do
ghosts like to listen to?
Soul music.

What organization do
girl ghosts join?
The Ghoul Guides.

Who began the Ghoul Guides?
Lord and Lady Baden-Howl.

Which ghosts haunt hospitals?
Surgical spirits.

How did James Bond
feel when he saw a ghost?
Shaken, not stirred.

Why did the ghost dress up in
trendy jeans and a zip-up top?
He liked to think
he was ghoul.

How do
ghosts start
all their letters?
Tomb it may
concern ...

9

How do ghouls chase away
bad smells?
With scare freshener.

What does the crowd shout
when someone scores at a
ghostly football match?
'Ghoul!'

Where do ghouls put their drinks to
stop them marking the furniture?
On ghoasters.

What event do ghouls take part in
on Sports' Day?
The egg-and-spook race.

Where do ghouls put
their letters?
In the ghostbox.

What's fifty metres long,
filled with water and very ghostly?
An Olympic-sized
swimming ghoul.

What's a ghoul's favourite
party game?
Musical bumps in the night.

How do short-sighted
ghouls see properly?
They wear spectre-acles.

What's a ghoul's
favourite type of bird?
A scarecrow.

What sort of make-up
do ghouls wear?
Ma-scare-a.

13

Which of Shakespeare's plays
stars a ghost?
Romeo and Ghouliet.

How do ghosts send emails?
By comBOOter.

BOO!

How do ghosts get rich?
They buy and sell scares on the
Shock Exchange.

How do ghouls keep in touch?
By eeeeekmail.

EEK!

TOP TEN

1
Terror-fried eggs

2
Stake and kidney pie
(Dracula's fave)

3
Freak and potato soup

4
Ghost and marmalade

5
Ghoulash
(if you're feeling Hungary)

6
Pork cackling

SPOOKY MEALS

...AND FOR DESSERT...

Quivering jelly
with cowardy custard

Shockolate mousse

Demon meringue pie

10

Strawberries
and scream

WATCH OUT FOR WEREWOLVES

They're hairy, they're scary and
these jokes will make them howl!

What happened when
the vampire changed
into a werewolf?
His bark was worse
than his bite.

AWOOO-OO-O!

18

How do you make a
werewolf stew?
Keep him waiting
for hours.

Why was the werewolf
arrested at the butcher's?
He was caught
choplifting.

19

Why did the werewolf
go out in the moonlight?
He just fancied a change.

How does a werewolf
sign his letters?
Best vicious.

What do you get if you
cross Tinker Bell
with a werewolf?
A hairy fairy.

Did you hear about
the werewolf
popstar?
He was a howling
success.

What do you call a werewolf that's
gambled all its money away?
Paw.

What do you call a werewolf
that's tired of howling?
A weary wolf.

What's a werewolf's
favourite day of
the week?
Moonday.

'DOCTOR, DOCTOR!'

Invisible man:
'Doctor, Doctor, everyone
keeps ignoring me!'
Doctor: 'Next, please.'

'Doctor, Doctor,
I feel like a witch's hat!'
'I see your point.'

'Doctor, Doctor,
I feel like a vampire!'
'Necks, please.'

'Doctor, Doctor,
I feel like a witch's broomstick!'
'There's no need to get
all bristly with me!'

'Doctor, Doctor,
I can't help scaring people!'
'Arrgghhh!'

'Doctor, Doctor,
since I was a skeleton
everyone seems to ignore me!'
'Send in the
next patient, Nurse.
There's nobody here.'

23

MONSTER MIRTH

Under the bed, in the wardrobe,
these beastly belly laughs are
coming to get you . . .

Why did the quiet monster
drip-dry after his bath?
He'd run out of growls.

Which soap opera do
monsters like best?
BeastEnders.

What does a monster
get on his birthday?
Bumps in the night.

First Mountaineer:
'Have you ever seen the
Abominable Snowman?'
Second Mountaineer:
'Not yeti.'

What do monsters put in their
fountain pens?
Monsters' ink.

How do monsters frighten pilots?
With scare traffic control.

Which monster
picks his nose?
The bogeyman.

Did you hear the one
about the creature that
needed a cleaner?
It was the
Loch Mess monster.

What creature is always late?
The Clock Less monster.

What do a chicken and
a monster have in common?
They're both fowl.

How can you tell if there's
a monster under your bed?
Your nose touches the ceiling.

What's a monster's
favourite party game?
Swallow-the-leader.

Did you hear the one about
the monster who gobbled up a sofa
and two armchairs?
He had a suite tooth.

What does the Loch Ness monster
eat every Friday night?
Fish and ships.

Why couldn't the monster hunter
find anything?
He ran out of loch.

What's evil, ugly and goes
down-up-down?
A bungee-jumping monster.

What do monsters buy
at the supermarket?
Grosseries.

GUNGE
ORANGE FLAVOUR

GUNGE

GRIME
'n'
SLIME

GLOOP GLOOP

BOGEY
BITES
ECONOMY SIZE

Which monster is
green, muscly
and very, very grumpy?
The Incredible Sulk.

Which cartoon do
monsters like the best?
Lilo and Frankenstein's Stitch.

How did the monster
count to thirty-seven?
On his fingers.

What did the
Abominable Snowman eat
with his bolognaise sauce?
Spag-yeti.

DRESSING LIKE A MUMMY BY ITZA WRAP

REACHING THE HIGH NOTES BY B. ANN SHEE

HOW TO BE REALLY WICKED BY I. M. A. DEVILLE

LOSING WEIGHT BY S. KELLY TUNN

FANTASTIC SPELLS BY MADGE ICK

Y BOOKSHELF

COPING WITH FEAR BY TERRY FIED

SKELETONS UNCOVERED BY X. RAY

HOW TO UNDO SPELLS BY B. WITCHED

MAGICAL EXCLAMATIONS! BY G. WIZ

CONTACTING THE DEAD BY R. U. THERE

SPOOKY 'KNOCK, KNOCK' JOKES

'Knock, knock.'
'Who's there?'
'Boo.'
'Boo hoo?'
'There's no need to cry –
I'm only a ghost.'

'Knock, knock.'
'Who's there?'
'Witches.'
'Witches who?'
'Witches the way to the
Hallowe'en Party?'

'Knock, knock.'
'Who's there?'
'Wanda Witch.'
'Wanda Witch who?'
'Wanda Witch you a
Merry Christmas!'

'Knock, knock.'
'Who's there?'
'Roar.'
'Roar who?'
'Roarther cold
out here!'

'Knock, knock.'
'Who's there?'
'Wicked.'
'Wicked who?'
'Wicked have a smashing time
if you'd let me in!'

'Knock, knock.'
'Who's there?'
'Who.'
'Who who?'
'Whoaaaa-ha-HAAAAA!
Did I scare you?!'

'Knock, knock.'
'Who's there?'
'It's Hal.'
'Hal who?'
'It's Hallowe'en! Trick or treat?'

'Knock, knock.'
'Who's there?'
'Turner.'
'Turner who?'
'Turn around, there's a monster behind you!'

KNOCK, KNOCK!

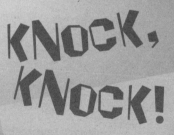

'Knock, knock.'
'Who's there?'
'Al.'
'Al who?'
'Al scream if you don't let me in!'

'Knock, knock.'
'Who's there?'
'Eve.'
'Eve who?'
'Evil – I'm totally evil!'

BEWARE OF BANSHEES!

They shriek, they moan,
they won't leave you alone . . .

Which country is
full of banshees?
Wales.

Did you hear the one about the
banshee who went to Hollywood?
She took a scream test.

What do banshees say to
each other when they can't
hear what's being said?
'Shriek up!'

When do banshees
do their shopping?
In the January wails.

What is a banshee's
favourite drink?
Whine.

Where do banshees go when
they are very young?
Noisery school.

Which soap opera
do banshees like best?
Coronation Screech.

What afternoon treat do
banshees enjoy in Devon?
A scream tea.

Where do banshee trainspotters
hang out?
At the wailway station.

41

TOP TEN

1. Arrrrgggght

2. English Witcherature

3. Germoan

4. Goregraphy

5. Hissstory

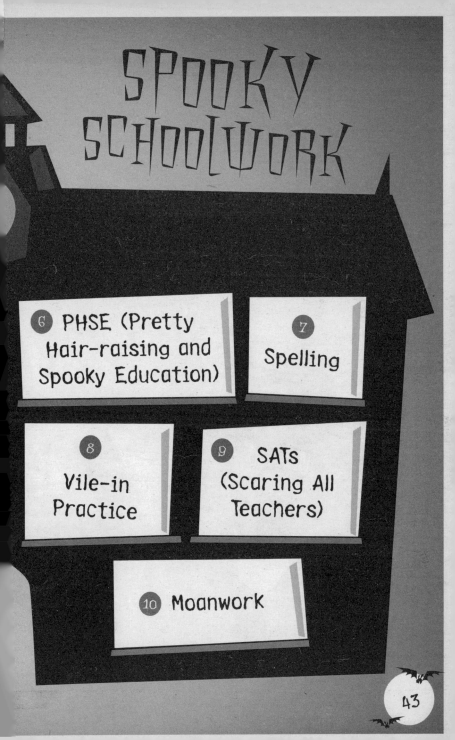

SPOOKY SCHOOLWORK

6 PHSE (Pretty Hair-raising and Spooky Education)

7 Spelling

8 Vile-in Practice

9 SATs (Scaring All Teachers)

10 Moanwork

43

DREADFUL
DEMONS

What possessed us to come up with
such devilishly bad jokes?

What does a
demon barber
give his customers?
A scarecut.

What happened
to the demon
with a broken shoe?
He lost his sole.

Why do you never find
a healthy demon?
They hate exorcise-ing.

What does a demon's
dessert taste like?
Devilicious.

What do demons use
to make toast?
Sliced dread.

What do devils drink?
Demonade.

Which percussion instrument
does a demon like to
rattle and shake?
The Satanbourine.

What's a demon's
favourite TV programme?
Fiends.

WICKED DAYS of THE WEEK

Which day of the week
do monsters bash people
over the head?
Stunday.

Which day of the week
do ghosts haunt people?
Moanday.

Which day of the week
do monsters eat people?
Chewsday.

Which day of the week
do vampires bite people?
Winceday.

Which day of the week
do vampires suck blood?
Thirstday.

Which day of the week
do monsters scare people?
Terrifriday.

Which day of the week
do witches land on people?
Splatterday.

WACKY WITCHES

We had to scrape the
bottom of our cauldrons
to find these wand-tastic jokes . . .

Why do trainee witches need
dictionaries?
Because they can't spell.

Why does a witch ride
on a broom?
A vacuum cleaner
is too heavy.

What is yellow on the outside
and wicked on the inside?
A witch dressed as a banana.

Why didn't the singing witch
hit the top note?
She couldn't screech it.

How do the speediest
witches travel?
By vroomstick.

What do witches use
on holiday?
Suntan potion.

What did the witch think
of the latest cloaks?
Wicked!

How do witches diet?
They go to
Weight Witches.

half
price!

What does a
good-weather witch do?
She forecasts sunny spells.

What does a witch
rest her teacup on?
A sorcerer.

Why do witches argue in shops?
They like to haggle.

What do young witches
do at school?

Spelling tests.

What noise does a
witch's fire make?

It cackles.

Why didn't the witch get upset
when she knocked over the
cat's saucer?

Because there's no use crying
over spelled milk.

What's a smelly sorceress
with pots of money?
Stinking witch.

How does a witch relax?
In a hubble bubble bath.

What do you call a witch
who tells the time without
moving her hands?
A digital witch.

Which scary person
cures spots?
Witch Hazel.

What do you call a witch
who sits in the middle lane
on the motorway?
A road hag.

How do witches
order food
in a hotel?
Broom service.

How did the witches
keep in touch?
With hex messaging.

How do witches make
their hair go wild?
With scarespray.

What sound does a witch's cereal make when she pours milk on it?
Snap, cackle and pop!

What do you call a witch when she's squashed between two slices of bread?
A sandwitch.

What should a witch on a broomstick never do?
Fly off the handle.

Why doesn't
a witch wear a
cowboy hat?
There's no point.

What's old, warty
and travels at
800 kilometres per hour?
A witch on a jet plane.

What did the witch
have for lunch?
A potion of soup.

What was the name
of the witch's mixing pot?
It was called Ron.

What kind of work do
magic-book printers do?
Spellbinding.

Did you hear the one about the French witch who worked as a chef? She gave the prince frog's legs.

What do you call the layer of air round Earth where witches fly? The atmosfear.

What's a witch's favourite fruit? Wartermelon.

What do witches put
on top of their hot chocolate?
Marshmallowe'ens.

Where do witches
warm their towels?
In a scaring cupboard.

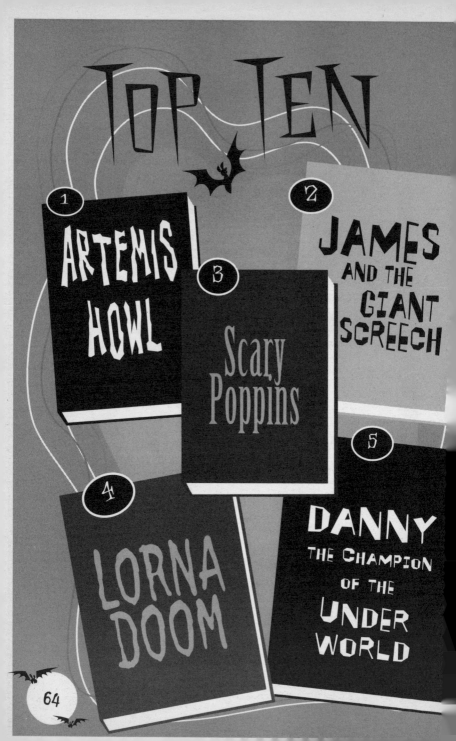

TOP TEN

1. ARTEMIS HOWL
2. JAMES AND THE GIANT SCREECH
3. Scary Poppins
4. LORNA DOOM
5. DANNY THE CHAMPION OF THE UNDER WORLD

SPOOKY BOOKS

6 The Howl who was Afraid of the Dark

7 Ghouldilocks and the Three Scares

WUTHERING FRIGHTS

10 CHARLIE and the SHOCKOLATE FACTORY

WINNIE THE BOO

9

HAUNTED HOUSE

Our friendly neighbourhood poltergeist is ready to welcome you – with some smashing jokes!

What did the jolly ghost hunter say when he persuaded people to go into a haunted house with him?
'That's the spirit!'

What keeps a haunted house cool during hot weather?
A fan-tom.

Who lights up a
haunted house?
The lights witch.

67

Did you hear the one about the
haunted clock radio?
It was alarmed.

What's yellow, scary
and sits on a beach?
A haunted sandcastle.

Who cleans a haunted school?
A scaretaker.

Did you hear the one about the haunted cartoon character?
His name was Spookemon.

What huge sparkly thing hangs from the ceiling and trembles?
A chandelfear.

GHASTLY GHOULS

More silly spooks to make you shake
with laughter!

Did you hear the one
about the ghostly comedian?
He was dead funny.

Which type of tune does
a ghost like best?
A haunting melody.

What do ghosts say when
they answer the door?
'Whooooooo is it?'

Where do
ghosts go
on holiday?
The Ghosta
del Sol.

Which of the
armed forces
do ghosts join?
The Terrortorial Army.

What happened
when the ghosts
went on strike?
A skeleton staff
took over.

Where do
North American
ghosts
do water sports?
Lake Eerie.

Where do ghosts
love to float about?
The Dead Sea.

Did you hear the one
about the ghost who
pressed the doorbell?
He was a
dead ringer.

Why couldn't the ghost
buy a glass of rum at the pub?
They didn't serve spirits.

What's the scariest ride
at a funfair?
The rollerghoster.

Where do ghost trains stop?
At devil crossings.

Why did the car stop
when it saw a ghost?
It had a nervous breakdown.

How do ghosts stay
safe in cars?
They wear a
sheetbelt.

Did you hear
the one about
the ghost who got lost
in the fog?
He was mist.

What do little ghosts
like for tea?
Spookghetti hoops.

What happens
if they eat too much?
They get phantummy ache.

What do ghosts say
to each other
after midnight?
'Good moaning!'

Did you hear
the one about the ghost
dressed as Santa Claus?
He was the Christmas spirit.

What game do
baby ghosts love playing?
Peekaboo!

Which fans support
ghostly football teams?
Football phantoms.

What type of street do
ghosts live in?
Dead ends.

What do ghosts
have for breakfast?
Dreaded Wheat.

Did you hear the one about the
ghost who would believe anything?
He was ghoullible.

What do ghosts always
carry around with them?
A mobile groan.

How do you know if
a ghost is telling lies?
You can see right
through him.

TOP TEN

1. BURY

2. CHILLINGHAM FC

3. FRIGHTON AND HOVE ALBION

4. GOREQUAY

5. IPSWITCH

SPOOKY FOOTBALL TEAMS

6 LIVERGHOUL

7 SHEFFIEND UNITED

8 SPELLTIC

9 STAKE CITY

10 WEREWOLVERHAMPTON WANDERERS

CREEPY CREATURES

Beasts of land and air and sea,
all as spooky as can be!

What do birds sing on Hallowe'en?
'Twick or tweet.'

What do you call a female horse
that's scared of sunlight?
A nightmare.

What do you call a
small scary dog from
the north of England?
A Yorkshire Terror.

Which noisy bird
flies at night?
The howl.

What do you call a
haunted chicken?
A poultrygeist.

83

What do you call a duck
with fangs?
Count Quackula.

What do you call a tiger
that is easily frightened?
A scaredy-cat.

Which buzzing insects are
like the walking dead?
Zombees.

Where did the
computer-friendly spider live?
On a website.

Where did the HUGE,
computer-friendly spider live?
On the World Wide Web.

Seriously Spooky LONELY HEARTS

• Tall, dark stranger with shiny white teeth (flosses hourly) seeks non-garlic eater for moonlit evenings. Must wash behind ears and round neck regularly.

• Man with pointy hat seeks woman with equally pointy hat for magical evenings. Applicants must like black cats and be a whizz with a broom.

· Shy Scottish monster seeks companion for underwater hide-and-seek games. Apply to: Loch Ness.

· Loud, whingeing woman seeks wailing friend to keep her company. Must enjoy unexpected bouts of shrieking and bringing doom and gloom to people's lives.

· Evil, caped woman seeks friends to take part in fun cookery evenings with slightly out-of-the-ordinary ingredients. Only those with warts, hooked noses and beady eyes need apply.

SKELETON SILLINESS

They'll groan in their graves when they hear our rib-tickling ripostes!

Why was the skeleton
at the disco lonely?
He had no body
to dance with.

Did you hear about
the skeleton who leaned against
the igloo wall?
It was spine-chilling.

What do skeletons carry when
they're on the move?
Mobile bones.

What does a skeleton pour
on to her Sunday roast?
Grave-y.

Did you hear about
the lazy skeleton?
He was bone idle.

Where's the
cemetery?
The dead centre
of town.

Did you hear the one about
the skeleton who made an
instrument out of his ribs?
He played the xylobone.

Why don't skeletons play
music in church?
They have no organs.

Why wouldn't
the skeleton bungee jump?
She didn't have the guts.

Why did the undertakers
drive round
the indoor arena?
They were at the
Hearse of the Year Show.

What do French skeletons
say before a meal?
'Bone appetit.'

Did you hear
the one about the three
skeletons up to
their ankles in mud?
They were six feet underground.

Why did the skeleton
give up modelling?
He didn't have the
body for it.

Did you hear
the one about the coffin
with the heavy bones inside?
It weighed a skeletonne.

Where do skeletons study?
At skull.

Did you hear
the one about the bulldozers
digging up the cemetery?
It was a grave situation.

How do old skeletons
play music?
On a gramobone.

What do you get
if you leave a pile of bones
lying on deckchair?
A skeletan.

Why aren't there any
celebrity skeletons?
Because they're
just a load of
nobodies.

Dear Doctor Dread,
I'm an incredibly evil demon
who used to enjoy terrifying
the neighbourhood with my
exceptionally evil demon friend.
But now we've fallen out and it's
no fun being bad on my own.
What should I do?

Be fiends, not enemies!

Dear Doctor Dread,
I'm a green, warty monster.
I smell awful. I'm ugly.
My cave needs a makeover.
They don't make fashionable shoes
in my size. I don't really like
being a monster anyway.
It's boring. And lonely ...
(and on and on and on ...)

You need a change of direction.
With all that moaning you'd make
an excellent ghost.

Dear Doctor Dread,
My friends think I'm weird because I don't like seeing ghosts and vampires on the TV.
That's not weird.
It makes me cross when they jump on my TV too!

Dear Doctor Dread,
I'm looking for the perfect ghostly boyfriend. He's got to be scarily handsome, almost see-through and dead funny. Where can I find him?
Ah, I see. You're looking for Mr Fright.

Dear Doctor Dread,
    I spend most of my
time in a coffin (the sun plays
havoc with my complexion), but
it makes me dreadfully cross
being cooped up in such a small
place. What should I do?
    Get rid of your anger —
flip your lid more often!

CROSSING-THE-ROAD JOKES

Beware – these jokes are HAZARDOUS!

Why didn't the ghostly bird
cross the road?

Because he was chicken.

Why did the witch cross the road?

Because she was stapled
to the chicken.

Why did the monster
cross the road?

Because he wasn't
chicken.

Why was the banshee too scared
to cross the road?
Because she
was yeller.

Why did the vampire stay
on the same side of the road?
He didn't like
crossing.

WALK,
DON'T
FLAP

THEY CAME FROM OUTER SPACE BY HAILEY ENN

THE DARK, SPOOKY NIGHT BY R. MAFFRAID

STITCHING FOR BEGINNERS BY FRANK N. STEIN

THINGS THAT GO BUMP IN THE NIGHT BY AL ARMING

ZOMBIE ALERT BY B. WARE AND B. HIND-YOU

THE INDECISIVE VAMPIRE BY WOODY BITE

EXPLORING HAUNTED HOUSES BY HUGO FIRST

THE ESSENTIAL GUIDE TO DEVILS BY D. MUNN

THE UNKNOWN GHOST BY MISS TREE

HOW TO SPOT A MAGICAL PERSON BY R. U. A. WIZARD

'VONDERFUL' VAMPIRES

Jokes you can really get your teeth into!

What dance do vampires do?
The fango.

Why do vampires always
dance in couples?
It takes two to fango.

Why did the vampire's
victim turn orange?
He'd been Fangoed.

What happens to people that Dracula attacks?

They're out for the Count.

What's a vampire's least favourite meal?

Steak.

Where do vampires
keep their savings?
In a blood bank.

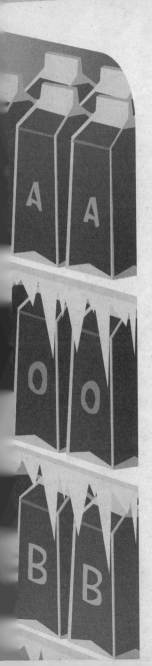

Why do vampires
have no friends?
Because
they're a pain
in the neck.

What do you call a
very short vampire?
A pain
in the knee.

Which type of dogs
do vampires own?
Bloodhounds.

How do you know when
Dracula's got a cold?
His coffin.

What do you call a
vampire who writes
TV dramas?
A scryptwriter.

What do you call a
vampire who writes for
the theatre?
A playfright.

Which type of crossword
does a vampire prefer?
One with **cryptic** clues.

What do American
vampires celebrate in
November?
Fangsgiving.

What does Dracula eat in
front of the TV on a
Friday night?
A **stake**away.

Why is maths
Dracula's
favourite activity?
He likes to Count.

What did the vampire say
when the ghoul admired
his teeth?
'Fangs.'

What do you call
a vampire who works at
the Kennedy Space Centre?
Countdown Dracula.

Why did the vampire eat
at the drive-through restaurant?
He fancied a quick bite.

Why did the vampire
sneak out in the daytime?
He fancied a light bite.

Where does Count Dracula
stay on holiday?
At a **vamp**site.

What has pointy teeth,
a high collar and a blue face?
A vampire holding his breath.

How did the vampire travel
across the sea?
In a **blood** vessel.

Which word game do
vampires like to play?
Fangman.

What's a vampire's
favourite type of fruit?
A necktarine.

What's a vampire's favourite sport?
Casketball.

Why did the vampire keep staring
at himself in the mirror?
Because he
was vein.

WILY WIZARDS

You'll laugh so much you'll need to lie down for a spell!

What do you call
an Australian wizard?
The Wizard of Oz.

What do you call an
unidentified wizard
zooming through the
night sky?
A flying sorcerer.

What do you call a
really speedy sorcerer?
A whizzard.

What do you call a
magical youngster who's
good with PCs?
A computer
whizzard-kid.

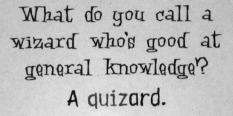

What do you call a
wizard who's good at
general knowledge?
A quizard.

What does a wizard
wear when he visits
friends in hospital?
A wardrobe.

Top Ten

1. 100 metres beaststroke

2. Batminton

3. Hearse racing

4. Hide-and-shriek

5. Moanopoly

SPOOKY SPORTS AND GAMES

117

SCARILY BAD JOKES

A selection of spellbindingly silly sidesplitters!

How do vampires
keep their drinks cold?
In a Dracooler box.

Did you hear about the
Mexican skeleton who had
too many bones?
He had spare ribs.

What do mummies like
to sing along to?
Wrap music.

What did the tomb raider shout
when the tomb creaked open?
'Mummy!'

119

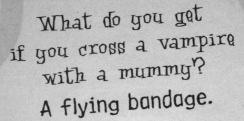

What do you get
if you cross a vampire
with a mummy?
A flying bandage.

What happened when
the two ghosts saw each other
at the Valentine's Ball?
It was love at first fright.

What do you get when
you catch phantom flu?
Fearache.

What does a witch
say to her friend Ian
on 31 October?
'Hallo, Ian!'

What do you call
a skeleton that won't work?
Lazy bones.

What kind of
mistakes do ghosts make?
Boo boos.

Did you hear the one
about the spooky
physics professor?
He was the seance teacher.